nickelodeon™

Look and Find®

TEENAGE MUTANT NINJA TURTLES™

Illustrated by Niño Navarra and Patrick Spaziante

 publications international, ltd.

Happy Mutation Day, Ninja Turtles! It has been 15 years since Leonardo and his brothers were mutated into ninja turtles, and Master Splinter was mutated into a rat. While the happy family celebrates, look around their underground lair for their ninja weapons.

Sais

Staff

Nunchuks

Bo staff

Ninja star

Katana

The Turtles face off against Shredder, Master Splinter's archenemy! Shredder and his Foot Clan have cornered the Turtles on the empty city streets, and it's time to kick some shell. Look around for these different ninja weapons.

Shredder's claws

Foot Clan throwing star

Water balloon

Tanto

Tegaki

Eggshell bombs

When the sun comes up, Splinter and the Turtles make sure to stay in the shadows. They can't reveal their secret identities! Search the city streets for our four heroes and their master, and see if you can also spot their good friend, April O'Neil, as well as Raph's pet turtle, Spike.

Raphael

Donatello

Michelangelo

Spike

Leonardo

April

Splinter

The streets of New York can be pretty dangerous, especially when evil villains are out to cause trouble. Help our heroes tackle these bad guys before they get away!

Baxter Stockman

Spider Bytes

Snakeweed

Fishface

Purple Dragon leader

Dogpound

The Kraang are an alien species out to cause harm to innocent civilians. The Turtles speed to the rescue with their awesome vehicles. See if you can spot the Kraang, as well as the Turtles' teched-out modes of transportation.

Patrol Buggy

This Kraang-droid

This Kraang

Skateboard

Stealth Bike

The Shellraiser

The Turtles were ready to enjoy a little pizza, but Baxter Stockman has a bone to pick with them. This time he's brought an army of mousers to beat our heroes! While the boys battle Baxter, look out for all these mousers!

With Baxter beaten, it's time for the Turtles to let loose. And what better way than hitting the skate park! While the fearless foursome ollie, kick-flip, and grind their way across the city, look for these other gnarly ways to get around.

Bicycle

Snowboard

Roller skate

Scooter

Unicycle

Pogo stick

The Turtles may have won a few battles, but the war has just begun! Not only is Shredder back, but the Kraang have returned, and the rest of our heroes' enemies have joined the fight, too. Look for these bad guys and help the Turtles take them down!

Fishface

Shredder

Dogpound

This Kraang

This Kraang-droid

Karai

Go back to the Turtles' awesome party and find 15 birthday candles hidden around the lair.

Race back to the fight with Shredder and his Foot Clan and see if you can spot these other weapons.

Scythe

Jitte

Mace

Ax

Blowgun

Suction-cup arrow

Tour the city during the day and find these New York City items.

Empire State Building postcard

Bagel

Hot dog

Statue of Liberty souvenir statuette

FDNY helmet

Newspaper

Make your way back into the city at night and look for these Purple Dragon gang members trying to get away with crimes.

Poaching a pooch's collar

Picking a pocket

Spraying graffiti

Burglarizing a cop's badge

Jumping a jogger

Snatching a purse

Speed back to the battle with the alien enemies and find six matching pairs of Kraang-droids. Look closely – they're almost all indentical!

Zoom through the city streets and find these silly types of pizza that Baxter's mousers scattered all around.

Turtle-shaped pizza

Cheese pizza

Fish pizza

Mushroom pizza

Birthday pizza

Candy pizza

Skate back to the park and look out for these not-so-awesome obstacles.

Mousetrap

Banana peel

Cream pie

Open manhole

Flimsy fire escape

Quicksand

Charge back into the battle and find these villains the Turtles must defeat!

Dr. Falco

Spider Bytes

Purple Dragon leader

Baxter Stockman

This Foot Ninja

Snakeweed